THROUGH THE MEDICINE CABINET

I was sure my dental brace was in the medicine cabinet in the bathroom, instead of in my mouth where it should have been. I got up and opened the door of the medicine cabinet. Yes! There was my brace. But then, just as I was about to close the cabinet door, something weird happened. Something very weird. The back of the medicine cabinet opened. And there, staring right in my face, was a boy . . .

THE ZACK FILES

THE ZACK FILES

FILES

THROUGH THE MEDICINE CABINET

DAN GREENBURG

Illustrated by
JACK E. DAVIS

MACMILLAN CHILDREN'S BOOKS

For Judith, and for the real Zack,
with love – DG

Copyright © 1996 by Dan Greenburg. All rights reserved.
First published in the United States by Grosset & Dunlap.
British publication rights arranged with Sheldon Fogelman.
First published in the UK 1997 by Macmillan Children's Books
a division of Macmillan Publishers Limited
25 Eccleston Place, London SW1W 9NF
and Basingstoke

Associated companies throughout the world

ISBN 0 330 35353 5

Illustrations © Jack E Davis 1996

The right of Dan Greenburg to be identified as the
author of this work has been asserted by him in accordance
with the Copyright, Designs and Patents Act 1988

1 3 5 7 9 8 6 4 2

A CIP catalogue record for this book is available fron the British Library

Typeset in Baskerville MT
Printed and bound in Great Britain by Mackays of Chatham plc, Kent

Chapter
One

● ● ● ● ●

I'm what you'd call a pretty normal kid. My name is Zack, which is a pretty normal name. I'm ten years old, which is a pretty normal age. I have normal brown hair and eyes. I have slightly crooked teeth, which is normal at my age. And I live in a big apartment building in New York. I always *thought* my building was normal, at least until the thing I'm about to tell you happened.

I've got to admit I've always been interested in weird stuff. Stuff like dead people crawling out of their graves at night. Or guys who stare at you and then suddenly their heads explode. I haven't actually seen those things. But who am I to say they couldn't happen?

Anyway, the time I want to tell you about happened at the beginning of spring vacation. My dad arranged to take me down to Florida. We were going to visit the New York Yankees at their spring training camp.

My parents are divorced. Part of the time I live with my dad. He's a writer, and he gets to do lots of cool things. Like go to spring training and then write about it in a magazine. I can't believe he gets paid to do this stuff. Neither can he.

Saturday morning was when we were planning to leave. I was so excited, I woke up at about 6 a.m. The minute I opened my eyes, I realized something. I had forgotten to put my dental brace in my mouth before I went to sleep. Where the heck was it?

A dental brace, in case you don't know, is a thing that you wear on your teeth at night. I don't exactly love my brace. It's made of wire and pink plastic. It's really gross-looking, especially when you take it out and put it on the table at lunch.

My dad hates it when I lose my brace They cost twelve hundred dollars, I think. Or a hundred and twelve. I forget which.

I left one brace in a pair of jeans, which went in the laundry. It melted to the inside of the pocket. One got chewed up in my Grandma Leah's garbage disposal. Another got flushed down the toilet. Another one I'm almost positive a robber stole while I was out of my room, although I've never been able to prove this.

All in all, I have not lost more than seven of them. Eight, tops.

I was sure my brace was in the medicine cabinet in the bathroom, instead of in my mouth, where it should have been. I got up and opened the door of the medicine cabinet. Yes! There was my brace. But then, just as I was about to close the cabinet door, something weird happened. Something very weird. The back of the medicine cabinet opened. And there, staring right in my face, was a boy who looked almost exactly like me!

Chapter Two

● ● ● ● ●

A boy who looked just like me? How could that be? I was so startled, I knocked over my brace. It fell into his bathroom. Then we both screamed and slammed our medicine cabinet doors shut.

What the heck was happening here?

Very slowly I opened the medicine cabinet again. Nope. There was nobody on the other side. I pushed against the back of it. It didn't open. Very weird.

So where was my brace? I figured I'd better check out the apartment next door. An old lady named Mrs Taradash lives there.

Mrs Taradash is kind of cranky. I know she isn't too happy about the basketball hoop I have mounted on my wall. She's complained to my dad lots of times. When I slam-dunk, she says it's like a 5.7 tremor on the Richter scale.

But maybe Mrs Taradash had a grandson. Maybe her grandson looked almost exactly like me. And maybe her medicine cabinet was hooked up to ours on the other side.

I knew this explanation didn't make

much sense. But it was all I could come up with.

I got dressed. Then I slipped quietly out of our apartment. I knocked on Mrs Taradash's door. There was no answer. I knocked again. It took a while before somebody opened it. Mrs Taradash was in a fuzzy robe and fuzzy slippers. Her hair was all messed up. And she was rubbing her eyes. She didn't seem all that thrilled to see me, if you want to know the truth.

"I'm sorry to bother you, Mrs Taradash," I said. "I was wondering whether I could get my brace out of your bathroom."

"Your what, precious?" she said.

She calls all kids precious. But you can tell she doesn't think they are.

"My brace," I said.

"What in the name of heaven is that, precious?"

"A brace is a thing made out of wire and pink plastic, which sometimes falls down disposals or toilets," I explained. "Mine fell into your apartment when your grandson opened the medicine cabinet door."

Mrs Taradash looked at me like I was cuckoo.

"I don't have a grandson, precious," she said.

"You don't have a grandson? Then who opened the other side of my medicine cabinet just now?"

The bottom half of her face smiled. But the top half was frowning. It looked like both halves were fighting with each other. She tried to close the door on my foot.

"Please don't close the door, Mrs Taradash," I begged her. "I lost my brace in your apartment. It's the eighth one that's got away from me. Maybe the ninth. If I don't get it back, my dad will kill me. You wouldn't want that on your conscience, would you?"

She opened the door and looked at me.

"What do you want?" she said. It was more hissing than talking. And she seemed to have forgotten the word "precious".

"Just my brace," I said, "which the boy who's not your grandson will tell you fell into your bathroom from my medicine cabinet. Please just let me look for it."

"If I let you look," she said, "will you go away and let me get back to sleep?"

"Yes, ma'am," I said.

She sighed a deep sigh. Then she waved me into the apartment.

I went in.

Weird. Everywhere you looked, there were stuffed animals. And I don't mean cuddly teddy bears, either. I mean real dead animals that were stuffed by a taxidermist. Squirrels, rabbits, beavers, chipmunks. They were all frozen in weird poses. And they stared at you through their beady glass eyes. They really gave me the creeps.

I hurried into the bathroom and looked around. There was no brace on the floor or anywhere else. I opened the medicine cabinet. I pushed against the back. It didn't budge. So I closed the medicine cabinet door.

"Satisfied?" she hissed.

I had a sudden feeling that if I didn't leave, her eyes would start glowing red. Then she'd grab me and try to stuff me. There I'd be, standing alongside the other animals in a weird frozen pose, staring at visitors through beady glass eyes.

I apologized and hotfooted it back to my dad's apartment. I didn't have a clue what had happened. I began to think I'd dreamed the whole thing. But if I did, then where was my brace?

On the way back to my bedroom, I passed my bathroom. Out of the corner of my eye I thought I saw something.

My medicine cabinet door.

It was slowly creeping open.

Chapter Three

● ● ● ● ●

I raced into my bathroom. I yanked open the door of the medicine cabinet all the way.

There he was! The same boy I'd seen before.

"Hey!" I said.

He didn't slam the door this time. I think he was too stunned. He kept staring. I was staring too. He really did look a whole lot like me. Only his teeth were a lot more crooked.

"Who are you?" I asked.

"Zeke," he said.

"I'm Zack."

"I know."

"You don't live next door," I said. "Do you?"

He shook his head.

"Then where do you live?"

"Somewhere else. Somewhere near by, but kind of far away, too. Somewhere you might think is weird."

"You live in New Jersey?"

He shook his head.

"Then where?"

"Have you ever heard of Newer York?" he said.

"Is that up near Poughkeepsie?" I asked.

He sighed and rolled his eyes like I had just said the stupidest thing in the world. I had a sudden thought.

"Hey," I said, "is this something really weird that I'm going to be sorry I got myself involved in?"

"I have time for just one more question," he said. "And then I have to go."

"OK," I said. "Do you have my brace? I think it fell on your side."

He suddenly tried to slam the door. But I was too fast for him. I stuck my arm into the medicine cabinet. That stopped him from shutting it. He grabbed my hand and tried to pry it off the door. I grabbed his wrist.

"Let go!" he shouted.

"Not till you give me my brace!"

He tried to pull away. I held on tight.

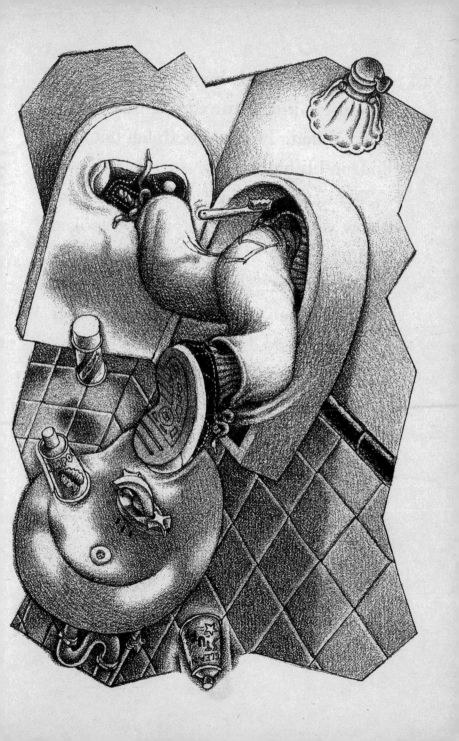

He backed up. I hung on with both hands. He pulled me through the medicine cabinet. Then we both fell onto the floor in his bathroom.

"Now you've done it!" he shouted. "Now you've really done it!" He looked frightened.

"Done what?" I asked.

"The one thing nobody is ever supposed to do," he said.

"What's that?" I asked.

"Cross over into a parallel universe!"

Chapter Four

• • • • •

"**W**hat the heck is a parallel universe?" I asked.

Zeke looked around nervously. "Shhhh!" he shouted. "Somebody might hear you!"

"You're the one who's shouting," I said. "What the heck is a parallel universe?"

"Well, it's kind of like this," said Zeke.

"Our universe is right next to yours. It's so close you wouldn't believe it. It even takes up some of the same space as yours. Only you can't usually see us. Except on Opening Days. Like today."

"Today isn't Opening Day," I said. "The baseball season doesn't start for a couple of months yet."

Zeke sighed and shook his head.

"The kind of Opening Day I'm talking about," he said, "has nothing to do with baseball. It's when your universe and mine move right next to each other. It doesn't happen a lot. It'll be years before it happens again."

"Sort of like an eclipse?" I asked.

"Sort of," he said. "When it's Opening Day, we can look through certain openings, like a medicine cabinet. Then we can see your universe. Which, by the way, isn't any better than ours."

"I didn't say it was better," I said. "Did I say it was better?"

"Maybe not. But I bet that's what you were thinking," he said. "We've got everything you've got. And it's just as good, believe me. Maybe even better."

"OK, OK!" I said. Then I picked myself up off the floor. I got my first good look at the parallel universe in Zeke's bathroom.

Hmmmm.

It looked pretty much the same as mine. Only different. First of all, there was something odd about the sink. There were two taps. But they were marked Cold and Not So Cold.

Then I looked at the roll of toilet

paper by the toilet. It looked like sandpaper. I hoped I wouldn't be in the parallel universe long enough to have to use the bathroom.

I noticed there was a lot of water on the floor. When I glanced at the shower I saw why. Instead of a shower curtain, there were venetian blinds.

"So what's Newer York like?" I asked.

"Outstanding," he said.

"How many channels do you get on TV?" I asked.

He looked at me suspiciously.

"You get more than one channel?" he asked.

"Never mind," I said.

"Hey," he said. "Everything in the Big Banana is as good as anything you've got in New York."

"Oh, you call Newer York the Big Banana," I said. "Like we call New York the Big Apple."

"Bananas are a lot cooler fruit than apples," he said.

"Look," I said, "I'm sure everything in your universe is every bit as cool as ours, OK? Now can I have my brace? And then will you please help me cross back over?"

"Zeke, are you packing?" The voice sounded a lot like my dad's.

"Yeah, Dad!" Zeke called back.

"Well, hurry up! The cab is coming at eight."

I looked at Zeke strangely.

"You're going somewhere with your dad?" I asked.

"Yeah. We have to catch a plane."

I got a sudden dizzy feeling.

"Your dad isn't by any chance taking you to the training camp of the New York Yankees, is he?" I asked.

"No."

"Well, *that's* a relief," I said.

"He's taking me to the training camp of the Newer York Yunkees. They're a triple-A minor league team. But they're just as good as the Yankees."

"Oh my gosh," I said softly. "Your life is just the same as mine, except a little different, isn't it?"

"Well, duh!" he said. "That's what a parallel universe is, Zack." He sounded like he was talking to a fourth-grader. I didn't appreciate that, since I happen to be in the fifth grade. "You want to know the truth? I'm a little tired of living in the one that's the copy and not the one that's the original."

"You are? But you just said——"

"Never mind what I said. I may live in a parallel universe. But I'm not stupid. Don't you think I'd rather be going to see the Yankees train than the Yunkees?"

"I can't hear you, Zeke!" called his dad. "Are you talking to me?"

"No, to myself!" he shouted. Then to me he said, "Hey, I've got an idea. Why don't we switch places? I'll go to the Yankees' training camp with your dad. You can go to the Yunkees' with mine."

"No way," I said.

"Never mind," he said. "I didn't want to do it anyway."

"Have you packed your brace yet?" called Zeke's dad.

"Don't worry about it!" Zeke answered nervously.

"Oh my gosh," I said. "Don't tell me you can't find your brace either!"

"So what?" he said.

This was freaking me out.

"Zeke," called his dad. He sounded like he was right outside the door. "Are you in there?"

Zeke looked scared.

"We can't let him see you here," he whispered. "You've got to hide!"

"Where?"

"Here."

He led me to the bathtub. He pulled back the blinds and pushed me inside. Then I heard him open and close the medicine cabinet door. And then nothing. What was he up to?

I looked at my watch. I had only a half hour before our cab came. What was I doing hiding in a bathtub in a parallel universe? And how was I ever going to get back to mine?

I peeked through the blind. Zeke was nowhere in sight. And then I knew.

That little rat had sneaked back through the medicine cabinet door into my universe!

Chapter
Five

● ● ● ● ●

I was in a panic.

At this very minute, Zeke was pretending to be me. He was getting ready to leave with my dad for the Yankee training camp in Florida!

I heard a knock at the bathroom door.

"Zeke, did you hear me? Are you ready?" said his father's voice.

I held my breath.

The door opened. Zeke's father came into the bathroom. Just then I sneezed.

"Achooooo!"

"Zeke? Are you in the shower?"

"No, sir," I said.

The blinds were pulled up. There stood a dad who looked almost exactly like mine.

At first I was scared he might be mad at me. But then he began to laugh.

"What are you doing in the shower with your clothes on?" he asked.

"Resting," I said.

"There's no time for resting, Zeke. Our cab is coming in about half an hour. Have you got your brace? Are you all packed?"

"Pretty much," I said.

He looked at me oddly and frowned.

"You look a little different, son. Did you comb your hair a new way this morning?"

"Yes, sir. I did. That's exactly what I did."

"Uh huh. OK. Well, I still have a few things to do. Zeke, could you run to the dry cleaners quickly and pick up all our cleaning?"

The cleaners! The only place I wanted to go was back through the medicine cabinet. But what could I say?

"Uh, s-sure," I stammered. "What cleaners would that be again?"

"You know. The one across the street and down the block."

"Uh huh. And what block would that be again?"

He looked at me and raised an eyebrow.

"C'mon," he said. "You've gone there

lots of times. Just get going. We have to leave soon.

"OK," I said.

He handed me a receipt and a twenty-dollar bill. Then he walked out of the bathroom.

The twenty-dollar bill looked strange. It was enormous. And when I examined it closely, I saw that along the top it said "The Untied States of America". The picture on all the twenty-dollar bills I've seen is of Andrew Jackson. This one was of somebody with bushy hair, a beard, and nose-glasses. His name was Slappy Kupperman.

I left the apartment and went down in the elevator. Then I got outside. I wanted to get to the cleaners and back as fast as I could.

At the corner I waited for traffic to stop. It was taking for ever. Then I looked up at the traffic signal and I saw why. Instead of a red and a green light, there were four lights.

The lights said, "STOP", "NOT YET", "HOLD ON", and "OK, GO ALREADY".

Newer York sure was a weird place.

A big billboard to my right said, "WE LOVE NEWER YORK! JUST AS GOOD AS NEW YORK. MAYBE BETTER!" Well, I didn't think so. I wanted to get back to my own universe.

I did manage to find the cleaners. I got Zeke's dad's clothes. Then I beat it out of there. I went back down the block. But I must have got messed up somehow. Because when I got to the corner, the big

billboard should have been to my left. But it wasn't there at all.

I took a quick look around. Nothing looked familiar. Then I saw a big apartment building across the street. It had a fancy canopy. It looked a whole lot like one in my own neighbourhood in my own universe. The Beekman Arms Plaza Apartments. I thought maybe the doorman could help me find my way back to Zeke's. The problem was, I didn't even know Zeke's stupid address. All I knew was that it would probably be like mine. Only a little different.

I ran to the building. But there wasn't any doorman. In fact, there wasn't even any building! What I thought was a building was only a fake front, like a movie set. The bushes in front of it were made of green plastic. There was a tag on them. It said, "Realistic bushes. Last longer. Need less care. Better than real."

I gulped. I felt like I was in a dream. One of those really awful ones where, no matter how hard you try to get somewhere, you can't, and then you puke.

In the middle of the street I saw an open manhole. There were police barricades around it. Signs said, "DANGER ON OPENING DAYS! FALLING IN WOULD BE STUPID! ALSO PAINFUL! DID WE MENTION ILLEGAL?"

Hey! This could be another way to get back to my universe! If I couldn't find my way back to Zeke's and go through the medicine cabinet, maybe I could climb through here. Going through the sewers would be pretty gross, of course. But I didn't care. At least I'd come out on the right side.

I waited for the traffic light to change. Again it took for ever. Then I raced up to the manhole. Now was the time to make my move. But just as I stooped down, I felt a heavy hand on my shoulder.

I looked up. A big policeman was standing over me. He seemed kind of scary. But then I looked at the gun in his holster. It was a Super Soaker.

"You wouldn't want to get too close and fall into New York," he said. "Now would you, sonny?"

"Oh boy, sir. I sure wouldn't want to do that," I said.

We both laughed pretty hard at the

idea I'd want to do anything as stupid as fall into New York.

"Well then, step away from there," he said.

I did. He stayed right next to the manhole. I don't think he trusted me. But with his Super Soaker he didn't seem so scary any more. I decided to ask his help.

"Um, Officer," I said, "I'm kind of lost. I was on my way home. But I must have taken a wrong turn or something."

"What's your address, son?" he asked.

"My address?"

"Yes."

"Uh, well, I'm not exactly sure," I said. "I mean it seems to have temporarily slipped my mind."

"Your address has slipped your mind?"

"Temporarily."

He looked at me strangely. But he listened while I described Zeke's building.

"Oh, I know the one you mean," he said. "I'll take you there."

He took me by the hand. Then he led me down the block and around the corner.

There it was, Zeke's building! I thanked him all over the place, and then I took off. He was probably glad to get rid of me.

Right in front of Zeke's building was a news-stand. It was just like the one in front of my own building. On the front page of all the newspapers were big headlines:

"DANGER! OPENING DAY ARRIVES! CITIZENS WARNED NOT TO TAKE CHANCES!"

Danger? What danger? I picked up a paper and started to read.

"Today, in the early hours of the morning, citizens of Newer York will once again be able to peek through any of several openings and actually observe life in our sister universe. 'Do not attempt to cross over into the alternate universe!' warns Professor Roland Fenster at the Newer York Institute of Parallel Universes. 'The openings should appear somewhere in the vicinity of 6 a.m. They will then shut down tight again approximately two hours later. Once shut, they will not reopen for as many as thirty years. Thirty years would be one heck of a long time to spend in a universe that's rumoured to be better than ours, but isn't.' "

I looked at my watch. Yikes! It was 7.45 a.m. I had just fifteen minutes before the cab came and Zeke left for Florida with my dad. And before the doors to my universe slammed shut for thirty years!

I raced into Zeke's building.

Chapter Six

● ● ● ● ●

I arrived back in Zeke's apartment out of breath. I dropped Zeke's dad's cleaning in the hallway. I raced into the bathroom.

I pushed hard against the back of the medicine cabinet. But I couldn't make the darned thing budge. Zeke obviously knew more about travelling between universes than I did!

And then I heard somebody behind

me. I whirled around to find Zeke's dad looking at me strangely.

"Zeke," he said, "what are you doing?"

Should I tell him the truth? Could I trust him? Or was he the enemy? I didn't know. But time was running out. And I didn't see that I had much choice.

"Listen, sir," I said, "this is going to sound sort of incredible. But it's the truth, so help me."

"All right, Zeke," he said. "But make it fast. We have less than fifteen minutes before the cab comes."

"OK," I said. "First of all, I'm not your son, Zeke. I'm somebody else who looks just like him. And my name is Zack. I live in the parallel universe. My dad and I were getting ready to go to the

Yankees' training camp. Just like you and Zeke were getting ready to go to the Yunkees' training camp. Only I dropped my brace through the medicine cabinet. I lost it, the same as Zeke lost his."

Zeke's dad's mouth dropped open. He smacked his forehead with his hand.

"I can't be-lieve it!" he said.

"It's true, though, sir," I said. "I swear."

"Zeke has lost his brace?" he said in a dazed voice. "That's the tenth one so far this year."

Wow! Zeke was even worse than me!

"Do you know how much those things cost?" he asked.

"Either twelve hundred dollars or a hundred and twelve dollars," I said quickly. "But didn't you hear the other stuff I told you?"

"Yes, yes, yes. Of course I did," he said. "Your name is Zack. You live in the parallel universe on the other side of the medicine cabinet, blah, blah, blah."

"You don't believe me, do you?" I said.

"Why shouldn't I believe you?" he said. "Everybody in Newer York knows about your universe. It's not like it's a big secret or anything. And it isn't any better than ours either, by the way."

Boy, this was a touchy subject with these guys!

"I never said it was better," I said. "Look, sir, you seem to know a lot about parallel universes. So maybe you know how to slip back through the medicine cabinet to mine. Like Zeke did just now."

"Zeke?" he said. "He crossed over?"

I nodded. I really had Zeke's dad's attention now.

"But it's almost 7.50!" Zeke's dad smacked his forehead again. "At eight o'clock Opening Day will shut down completely!"

"My point exactly, sir," I said. "I'd be miserable if that happened. Not that I wouldn't love living here, I mean. Because I think it's at least as good as my universe. And maybe even better. But the thing is, I'd really miss my mom and dad."

"OK, OK," said Zeke's dad. "This is what you have to do. Put your hand on the back wall of the medicine cabinet."

I did.

"Close your eyes. Take a deep breath.

Now visualize the back wall opening. Let me know if you feel anything."

I did everything he said. It started to work. The wall was starting to feel kind of springy. I opened my eyes in time to see it sort of melt away.

Chapter Seven

● ● ● ● ●

"Hi, Zack," said a familiar face.

"Zeke!" said Zeke's dad. "Oh, thank heavens!"

"Zeke!" I said. "Were you coming back?"

He looked embarrassed.

"I got homesick," he said. "I mean, your dad is awfully nice, Zack. He really is. But he's not my dad. And this isn't my universe. I figured you must feel the same way. Even though Newer York is just as cool as New York."

My dad appeared on the other side of the medicine cabinet.

"Dad!" I said.

"Hi, Zack," said my dad. Then he turned to Zeke's dad. "Hi, Don," he said. "Long time, no see."

"Hi, Dan," said Zeke's dad to my dad.

They shook hands through the medicine cabinet.

"You two *know* each other?" I asked, amazed.

"Yeah, we met when we were your age," said Zeke's dad. "But it wasn't through a medicine cabinet. It was through a dryer in the laundromat."

"Yeah," said my dad. "I always

wondered what happened to odd socks that got lost in the laundry. Who'd have guessed they go to the parallel universe?"

"That was quite an Opening Day," said Zeke's dad. "Not much laundry got dried. But we sure had fun. Your dad thought I lived in the dryer."

Both my dad and Zeke's dad started laughing their heads off.

"Uh, excuse me for interrupting," I said. "This is all very interesting. But it's now 7.55."

"Oh, right, right!" said Zeke's dad. He looked through the cabinet at Zeke. "Do you still want to go to the Yunkees' training camp, son?"

"I sure do!" said Zeke.

"Then let me pull you through," said Zeke's dad.

So Zeke crawled back into his own universe. I crawled back into mine.

"I'm sorry, Zack," said Zeke. "I was a real jerk."

"You were," I said. "But I forgive you."

Cab horns were now honking on both sides of the cabinet.

"Well, so long, guys," I said.

"See you again sometime," said Zeke.

"Maybe at the next Opening Day," I said.

"OK," said Zeke.

He fished something out of his pocket. He handed it to me through the cabinet. It was my brace!

"You swiped my brace?" I said.

He nodded sheepishly.

"But I couldn't keep it," he said.

"Because you knew it was wrong."

"Yeah," he said. "Also, it didn't fit."

Then all of a sudden, the grandfather clock in our hallway started chiming.

It was eight o'clock.

We waved goodbye to each other. Then, instead of facing Zeke and his dad, I was looking at shelves with toothpaste and deodorant. I pushed hard against the back wall of the medicine cabinet. I visualized like crazy. But nothing happened.

So that's how I discovered the parallel universe. And every time I open my medicine cabinet, I think of Zeke and his dad. I kind of miss them. It's funny to think that they're so close, and yet so far away.

The next time I see Zeke, I could have

a son of my own. Weird! I wonder what he'll be like. Hey, wouldn't it be cool if he's just like me? In every way except one: I hope he doesn't ever need to wear a brace!

What else happens to Zack?

Find out in

A GHOST NAMED WANDA

One night a few months ago, I woke up suddenly. All the doors in our apartment kept on opening and closing. The door to Dad's room, my bedroom door, my bathroom door, the door to my closet. Just opening and closing by themselves. I figured, hey, no big deal. It's the wind or something. So I went back to sleep. If I had known what it really was, I probably wouldn't have been so casual . . .

THE ZACK FILES

All Macmillan titles can be ordered at your local bookshop
or are available by post from:

**Book Service by Post
PO Box 29, Douglas, Isle of Man IM99 1BO**

Credit cards accepted. For details:
Telephone: 01624 675137
Fax: 01624 670923
E-mail: bookshop@enterprise.net

Free postage and packing in the UK.
Overseas customers: add £1 per book (paperback)
and £3 per book (hardback).

The prices shown are correct at the time of going to press. However,
Macmillan Publishers reserve the right to show new retail prices on
covers which may differ from those previously advertised.